Solomon Leviathan's Nine Hundred and Thirty-First Trip Around the World

URSULA K. LE GUIN

Illustrated by Alicia Austin

Philomel Books

NEW YORK

Text copyright © 1983 by Ursula K. Le Guin. Illustrations copyright © 1988
by Alicia Austin. Published by Philomel Books, a division of The Putnam &
Grosset Group, 200 Madison Avenue, New York, NY 10016. All rights
reserved. Published simultaneously in Canada. Printed in Hong Kong by
South China Printing Co. Typography and lettering by Golda Laurens.

Library of Congress Cataloging-in-Publication Data

Le Guin, Ursula, K., 1929– Solomon Leviathan's nine hundred and thirty-
first trip around the world / Ursula K. Le Guin : illustrated by Alicia Austin.
p.   cm. Summary: A giraffe and a boa constrictor go to sea in a small boat
and are swallowed by Solomon Leviathan, the ancient whale who swallowed
Jonah and Pinocchio. [1. Animals—Fiction.   2.Fantasy.]   I. Austin, Alicia,
ill. II. Title.   III.   Title: Solomon Leviathan's 931st trip around the world.
[PZ7.L5215So 1988] [Fic]—dc19   87-16590 CIP AC ISBN 0-399-21491-7
First Impression

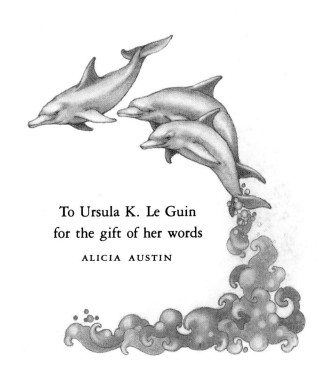

To Ursula K. Le Guin
for the gift of her words

ALICIA AUSTIN

long way from the coast of Kansas there is an island, a runcible island covered with forests. In the midst of the forests is a little clearing, a quiet place where the sun shines warm. A giraffe and a boa constrictor used to live there. They were philosophers, and they were friends. They do not live there any more, because one morning, after a long and thoughtful silence, the giraffe turned his head and spoke. "The sun's halfway to noon," he said.

"What?" said the boa constrictor with a start, which began at her nose and ran like a wave to the tip of her tail.

"Excuse me for startling you, but the sun's halfway to noon. It's time to go."

"Go where?" said the boa constrictor.

"To the sea," said the giraffe.

"Of course," said the boa constrictor, and they set off.

"I know a Rune about the sea," the giraffe said, after they had crossed several forested hills and valleys.

"It will be useful when we get there," the boa constrictor answered, as they climbed another hill.

"I admire the way you climb," said the giraffe. "I wish I could wriggle, I wish I could flow. Do you mind if I ask you a personal question?"

"Not at all, my friend."

"Where does your tail begin? Where does the rest of you leave off? Does your tail begin where the back of your head stops? That seems peculiar. But where does one draw the line?"

"My friend," said the boa constrictor, "I am an indivisible entity to which such hypotheses are irrelevant."

"I see," said the giraffe.

"Now I have a question," said the boa constrictor. "It is said of giraffes that they have no voice, but very keen eyesight. You, however, talk fluently, but while talking you frequently bump into trees, stumble over vines, and fall into puddles. Why is this?"

"My friend," said the giraffe, "I am an intellectual giraffe."

"I see," said the boa constrictor.

So, the one wriggling and flowing, the other striding and stumbling, the two friends came to the shore. They stood on the yellow sand and observed the sea. Close at hand it kept smashing itself to pieces on the sand, and the white broken bits of it scudded in the wind. Far off it looked quiet and green, and still farther off the green turned misty, and the blue sky above it turned misty, and they met in a mist.

"The horizon reminds me of your tail," said the giraffe. "I'm not sure where the sea stops and the sky starts, or the other way round."

"In the middle," said the boa constrictor.

"Is that true of your tail, too?"

"No," the boa constrictor said in her dry voice.

"Well," the giraffe said after a pause, "what now?"

"Try that Rune you mentioned."

The giraffe assumed the attitude proper to the recitation of Runes, and recited:

> *Cannot sail*
> *Cannot flail*
> *Cannot fail*
> *To be a whale.*

"Irrelevant, irrelevant," the boa constrictor said sternly; but the giraffe was peering at an object far down the beach.

"That's a boat," he said. "A boat is highly relevant."

"I'll get seasick," said the boa constrictor.

"I've never made a journey on the sea," the giraffe said in a wistful tone.

"You have never seen a seasick boa constrictor, either. Very few people have."

The giraffe looked wistful and said nothing, until the boa constrictor said, "Oh, very well."

They went down the beach and got into the little boat, which lay at the edge of the waves. The giraffe stood amidships, and the boa constrictor coiled herself neatly in the stern. After some while she said, "It's odd; I don't feel seasick."

"I suppose that's because the boat is still lying on the sand," the giraffe replied, but at that very moment the incoming tide sent a big wave up the beach, and the boat rose, rocked, and floated.

"Are you seasick?" the giraffe inquired with interest.

"Not yet," said his friend. "I feel well. I feel daring. I feel nautical. Ahoy!"

"Abaft the mainsails!" cried the giraffe. "Splice the forecastle! Starboard and hardtack! Ahoy!"

They soon noticed, however, that the boat was being carried out by the backwash and then carried back in by the next wave, so that they were not getting anywhere in particular.

"There are no oars," said the giraffe. "We can't row. We are lost! Abandon ship!"

"Never," said the boa constrictor. "A boa constrictor always goes down with the ship!" She uncoiled, took a firm hold on the stern with her mouth, lowered the rest

of herself into the water, and began to whirl herself rapidly—all but the head. This is how all big ships move themselves, although instead of a boa constrictor they use a rotary screw. The boat moved rapidly away from the shore, and before long it met a current which carried it off. The boa constrictor hauled herself aboard while the giraffe sang a capstan chanty; and they looked about. They were far out on the open sea.

"The sea is bluer than the sky," the giraffe said, looking down. "The sky is bluer than the sea," he said, looking up.

"Impossible," said the boa constrictor. "Of two things, one must be bluer."

"Not of two bananas," said the giraffe.

"Ahoy!" the boa constrictor shouted.

"Ahoy what?"

"Ahoy what's ahead of us!"

"There's nothing ahead of us at all except that mist where the sky and sea meet."

"I'm ahoying that. Isn't it worth ahoying?"

"Yes," said the giraffe, looking at the horizon. "Certainly. Ahoy, horizon!"

The horizon did not answer.

The boat drifted smoothly on.

"That horizon keeps the same distance from us," the giraffe said. "It's trying to run away."

"We shall pursue it," the boa constrictor said grimly.

"What shall we do when we reach it?"

"Order it to strike sail. Board it. Conquer it!"

"Hurray! Ahoy!" cried the giraffe. "Horizon, we are coming!"

They drifted on over the smooth blue swells in the sunlight.

"The sea is a friendly and delightful place," said the boa constrictor. "It is as peaceful as our clearing in the forest, and much larger." A long, dark cloud had appeared on the horizon.

"How quaint and imaginative," said the giraffe, "are the old myths and folktales of storms at sea!" At this moment the cloud rushed up the sky and overtook the sun.

"Childish stories," said the boa constrictor, "laughable to those who, like us, truly know the sea."

The sky was now purplish brown; the boat rocked and pitched as it climbed the steepening waves; and the wind whistled shrill past the giraffe's ears. A flash of lightning lighted the white wave-tops, the thunder roared, and rain poured down in sheets.

"Were we on land," said the boa constrictor, "I should almost call this a storm."

"My feet are wet," said the giraffe.

"Mine aren't," said the boa constrictor.

"This is not a storm at sea, of course," the giraffe said nervously, "but for some reason the boat is getting very full of water. I think we should get the water back into the sea."

"How?"

They looked about, but in the wild glare of the lightning they saw nothing but the water sloshing in the boat, and the rain sluicing out of the clouds, and the waves cavorting hugely all around.

"What does one usually do with water?" said the giraffe.

"One usually drinks it," said his friend.

They both sighed. The giraffe braced his long legs, lowered his long neck, and began to drink. The boa constrictor coiled herself up and began to drink.

"It tastes like bilge water!" the boa constrictor said indignantly.

"It is bilge water," the giraffe said.

They continued to drink. They drank, and drank, and drank; and the level of the water in the boat sank slowly,

plank by plank; and the thunder rolled away over the waves, and the sun shone through the tearing edges of the cloud. When at last the rain had stopped and there was no more water sloshing in the boat, the giraffe tried to raise his head, but it remained stuck straight out in front of him. The boa constrictor had come uncoiled and was also looking very stiff, straight, fat, and uncomfortable.

The sun shone warm again, and slowly they dried out. The giraffe raised his head, little by little, sloshing faintly. The boa constrictor coiled up little by little, muttering, "Bilge!"

The boat moved on over the sunlit sea.

Something rose up from the sea before them, white, like a fountain or a spray of white flowers.

"Ahoy!" the giraffe shouted, plunging with excitement.

"Don't rock the boat!" the boa constrictor cried, but before she had finished her words there was a loud yawning noise, a long sliding feeling, and a blackness.

The two friends, there in the blackness, said nothing for a while.

"Is this the horizon?" the giraffe murmured, doubtfully.

"You might try that Rune again," the boa constrictor said in her dry voice.

Once more the giraffe assumed the attitude proper to the recitation of Runes. Something dripped on his nose and something gurgled near his feet, but he ignored the drips and gurglings and recited:

> *Cannot sail*
> *Cannot flail*
> *Cannot fail*
> *To be whale.*

"Whale," said the boa constrictor in the darkness.
"Irrelevant!" the giraffe said, hopefully.

"Look," said the boa constrictor, and she pointed her nose at a pair of small spots of light, some distance from them. "Those little windows," she said, "are the whale's eyes."

"Oh, dear," said the giraffe. He stretched out his neck as far as it would go and peered out through one of the whale's eyes. He saw a depth of green water with a small fish swimming in it. The sight did not please him. He straightened up his neck and pondered for a minute.

"My friend," he said, "are we not philosophers?"

"Yes," said the boa constrictor, "we are."

"Then it is our duty to wait philosophically for whatever may happen," the giraffe said. He folded his long legs; the boa constrictor coiled herself neatly; and they waited philosophically for whatever might happen.

Around them, the whale went swimming through the sea. He had had a good nap and felt well. For a while he amused himself by pushing a loose island about through the water; then he chased a shoal of seventy thousand salmon to the mouth of a river, and watched them go leaping upstream. Salmon do this anyway, but the whale pretended they were afraid of him, and went off, flipping his tail and trying to leap like a salmon, which was uncomfortable for his passengers and unfitting to his

years. After this he swam up north and ate a small iceberg, and it got very cold inside him where the giraffe and the boa constrictor were. Finally he swam within sight of the coast of Switzerland, and there he stood on his head and began to swim down to the floor of the sea.

The light died out of the water as he swam down, till only blue was left, and then a dim violet, and finally no light at all: it was black, blacker than a room at midnight with the curtains drawn. But in the blackness were strange fish, who shone like Christmas-tree lights: white, yellow, green, and pink. They swam about, never blinking their huge, luminous eyes, but waving their long, fringed fins constantly in the heavy water. One of them came up to the whale and spoke to him; but the whale did not understand its language, and felt lonely down there at the underside of the sea.

The boa constrictor had heard the luminous fish speak, and being very learned she understood the language. "Did you hear that?" she cried. "That is the lost language of Mumatlan!"

"I don't know it," the giraffe replied, philosophically.

Now it was utterly silent in the depths of the sea, and the whale could hear the voices of the giraffe and the boa constrictor clearly, as he could not do on top of the sea,

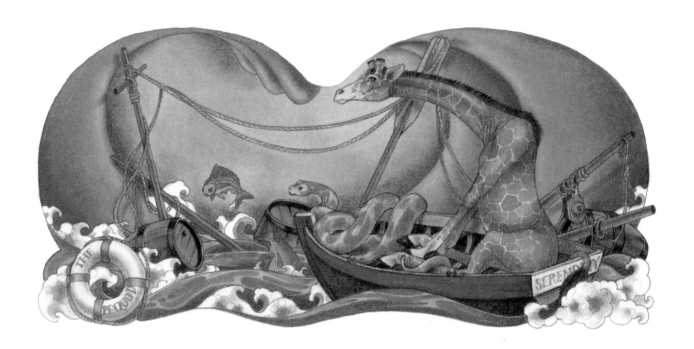

because of the sound of wind and waves. "Is somebody
there?" he asked in an eager tone. "I can't see you. Where
are you?"

"Inside," the boa constrictor said, and the giraffe
added, "About the third rib, I believe."

"How many of you?"

"Two."

"Good," said the whale in his deep voice, which
echoed wonderfully inside him, like an organ in a cathe-
dral. "Last time it was a whole boatload of sailors. They
chewed tobacco and spat. Before that it was a little
wooden puppet fellow; and a baron, whose name I didn't
catch; and then there was that fellow who started it all—
the one who argued so much—what was his name?

25

Jonah, that's it. I do hope you have made yourselves at home? My name is Solomon Leviathan."

"I am Damon, and my friend is named Ophidia," said the giraffe.

"Delighted to make your acquaintance," said the whale. "May I ask where you were going, when I inhaled you?"

"We were sailing to the horizon," the boa constrictor said.

"Sailing to the horizon!" said the whale, frightening away the luminous fish who had gathered to stare at him with their great bright eyes. "To the horizon! My friends, I was named after King Solomon, I am the second son of the first whale, I have swum round the world nine hundred and thirty times, and I have never reached the horizon!"

The giraffe and the boa constrictor were silent for a short while. At last the giraffe said, "Mr. Leviathan, you are older than anyone in the world, but because even you have never reached the horizon does not mean that it cannot be reached."

"I am not the eldest," the whale said slowly. "There is a redwood tree in California twice as old as I, and an elephant in India who is the first elephant that ever was.

Adam named him. Lord Buddha rode him. He might know about the horizon."

"Is it a long way to India?" asked the boa constrictor.

"Not since they made the Suez Canal," said the whale, and with a mighty blow of his tail he started off upward and eastward.

When he came to India he rose to the top of the sea and beat the water with his tail, making waves that crashed upon the beaches. Presently the jungle at the water's edge shook, and a little grey elephant came out. "How do you do, Solomon?" he said.

"Very well, thank you, Elephant," said the whale. "I have two passengers inside me, philosophers and friends. They wish to reach the horizon. Can you advise them?"

Elephant sighed. "The horizon," he said, "is an effect formed by the curve of the earth, the mist on the sea, and the beholding eye. The horizon is not a place. It does not exist. I do not know how to get there. If I were you, I should simply go ahead. It seems the best way."

"The horizon must exist," the whale said. "If we want to get to it, why then, it is the thing we want to get to. Is this true, Elephant?"

Elephant nodded. "That is why I recommend simply going ahead. You might try to avoid fog, but really that doesn't matter. Even in the fog one can imagine the horizon."

"We thank you, Elephant," said the whale; and he opened his mouth very wide so that the giraffe and the boa constrictor could stand under the great arc of his palate and say thank you too. Elephant raised his trunk in salute and went back into the jungle with a soft, slow pace.

"Well, my friends, shall we go ahead?" the whale asked.

"Certainly!" said the boa constrictor; and the giraffe said, "Mainbrace the stuns'ls! Full steam ahead!"

The whale turned from the coast and swam towards the horizon, with his mouth still open so that Damon and Ophidia could see out.

That was a long time ago. So far as anybody knows they are still swimming. At noon Solomon Leviathan stops by an island, and the giraffe and the boa constrictor get out and eat lunch, while the whale goes fishing. Along in the mid-afternoon he returns; they climb back in; he spouts, and they all set off toward the horizon. When he is tired he rests on the water. The two philosophers recite Runes and Odes, and the whale tells tales from History, such as the story of King Louis the Fourteenth, whom he once saw walking on a French beach with a crown and red high-heeled shoes on. When he is

rested, he swims on. The three friends have already been around the world; they have not caught up with the horizon yet, but they are having such a good time trying that they intend to go right on.